D0667092

Room Nine, Kindergarten Friends

Mrs.

Junie B. Jones

Richie Lucille

That Grace

Meanie Jim

Crybaby William

Paulie Allen Puffer

Jamal Hall

Ricardo

Roger

Charlotte

Lynnie

Laugh Out Loud with Junie B. Jones!

junie b. jones®
Has a Monster Under Her Bed

by BARBARA PARK

illustrated by
Denise Brunkus

A STEPPING STONE BOOK™

Random House 🏠 New York

Text copyright © 1997 by Barbara Park
Cover art and interior illustrations copyright © 1997 by Denise Brunkus

All rights reserved. Published in the United States by
Random House Children's Books, a division of Random House LLC,
a Penguin Random House Company, New York.

Random House and the colophon are registered trademarks and A Stepping Stone Book and the colophon are trademarks of Random House LLC. Junie B. Jones is a registered trademark of Barbara Park, used under license.

JunieBJones.com

Educators and librarians, for a variety of teaching tools, visit us at
RHTeachersLibrarians.com

Library of Congress Cataloging-in-Publication Data
Park, Barbara.
Junie B. Jones has a monster under her bed / by Barbara Park ;
illustrated by Denise Brunkus.
    p.   cm.   "A stepping stone book."
Summary: After hearing from a classmate at kindergarten that people have monsters under their beds, Junie B. Jones is afraid to go to sleep at night.
ISBN 978-0-679-86697-8 (pbk.) — ISBN 978-0-679-96697-5 (lib. bdg.) —
ISBN 978-0-307-75472-1 (ebook)
[1. Monsters—Fiction.   2. Bedtime—Fiction.   3. Fear—Fiction.
4. Kindergarten—Fiction.   5. Schools—Fiction.]   I. Brunkus, Denise, ill.   II. Title.
PZ7.P2197Jtw   1997   [Fic]—dc20   96-42561

Printed in the United States of America   59

This book has been officially leveled by using the F&P Text Level Gradient™ Leveling System.

Contents

1

The Cheese Man

My name is Junie B. Jones. The B stands for Beatrice. Except I don't like Beatrice. I just like B and that's all.

I am in the grade of afternoon kindergarten.

Today we got school pictures taken at that place.

School pictures is when you wear your bestest dress. And you go to the cafeteria. And a cheese man is there.

He makes you say *cheese*. Only I don't actually know why.

Then he takes pictures of you. And your mother has to buy them. Or else you will get your feelings hurt.

School pictures is a racket, I think.

I wore my new dress with the dinosaur on the front.

"A dinosaur, huh?" said the cheese man.

I smoothed my skirt very lovely.

"Yes," I said. "It is a Tyrannosaurus Dottie."

"You mean Tyrannosaurus *Rex,*" he said.

"No. I mean Tyrannosaurus Dottie. 'Cause Rex is the boy. And Dottie is the girl," I explained.

The cheese man stood behind his camera.

"Say *cheese,*" he told me.

"Yeah, only guess what? I don't actually know why I have to say that word. 'Cause what's cheese got to do with it?" I asked.

"Cheese makes you smile," said the cheese man.

I shook my head.

"Not *me*. Cheese doesn't make *me* smile," I said. "'Cause sometimes I eat a cheese sandwich for lunch. And I don't even giggle when I swallow that thing."

The cheese man did a big breath.

"Could you please just say it?" he asked.

"Yes," I said. "I can *please just say it*. Only don't forget to tell me when you're ready. 'Cause one time my grampa Frank Miller was taking my picture. And he didn't tell me he was ready. And then one of my eyes turned out opened. And the other one turned out closed."

I made the face to show him.

"See? See my eyes? See how one of them is opened and the other one is…"

All of a sudden, the cheese man took my picture.

My mouth came wide open at him.

"HEY! HOW COME YOU DID THAT? HOW COME YOU TOOK MY PIC-TURE? 'CAUSE I WASN'T EVEN READY YET!"

The cheese man kept on clicking his cam-era.

Pretty soon he looked at the next person in line.

"Next," he said.

I stamped my foot.

"Yeah, only I wasn't ready, I tell you! And so I need another turn!" I said.

Just then, my teacher came over. And

she pulled me away from there.

She sat me next to her on a bench.

Her name is Mrs.

She has another name, too. But I just like Mrs. and that's all.

Mrs. said *settle down* to me.

Then me and her watched the rest of the children get their pictures taken.

My bestest friend named Lucille went next.

She had a blue satin ribbon in her hair.

"My nanna says this ribbon brings out the blue in my eyes," she told the cheese man.

She opened them real wide.

"See them? See their color? They are robin's egg blue...with just a *hint* of lavender."

The cheese man sucked in his cheeks. He

was getting fusstration in him, I think.

"Could you please just say *cheese*," he grouched.

Lucille smiled real big with all her teeth.

"Cheese!" she sang very loud. "Cheese! Cheese! Cheesie, cheese, cheese!"

Then she kept on singing *cheese*, till the cheese man said, "Knock it off."

After she was done, Lucille skipped over to me and Mrs.

"Did you see me?" she asked. "Did you see how good I said *cheese*? That's because I'm going to be a model when I grow up. So I already know how."

She fluffed her fluffy hair.

"The camera is my friend," she said.

Mrs. rolled her eyes way up at the ceiling. I looked up there, too. But I didn't see anything.

After that, it was time for the class picture.

The class picture is when all of Room Nine lines up in two rows.

The biggie kids stand in the back. And

the shortie kids stand in the front.

I am a shortie kid. Only that is nothing to be ashamed of.

I stood next to Paulie Allen Puffer.

He looked very admiring at my dinosaur dress.

"Dinosaurs bite people's heads off," he said.

I did a frown.

"Yeah, only they don't even scare me. 'Cause there's no such things as dinosaurs anymore," I told him.

"So? There's still such things as monsters that can bite your head off," said Paulie Allen Puffer. "A monster lives right under your bed, I bet. My big brother says that *everybody* has a monster under their bed."

He poked his finger at me.

"Even *you*, Junie B. Jones," he said.

I got shivers on my arms.

"No, I do not either, Paulie Allen Puffer," I said.

"Yes, you do too," he said back. "My brother is in seventh grade. And he says the monster waits till you're asleep. Then he crawls up next to you. And he lies down on your pillow. And he practices fitting your head in his mouth."

I covered up my ears. But Paulie Allen Puffer talked louder.

"I can even *prove* it," he said. "Didn't you ever wake up with a drool spot on your pillow?"

I thought very hard.

"Yeah...so?"

"So where do you think it came from?" he asked. "It came from the *monster* under your bed, that's where. It was *monster* drool, Junie B. Jones."

I shook my head real fast.

"No it was not, Paulie Allen Puffer! You stop saying that! And I mean it!"

He raised up his eyebrows.

"Well, where did it come from then? *You* don't drool on your pillow. Do you? You're not a *baby*, are you?" he said.

"No! Don't call me that! I am not a baby!" I yelled.

Paulie Allen Puffer crossed his arms.

"So where did the drool come from then?" he asked again.

"I don't know," I said. "But my daddy told me there's no such things as monsters."

"So what? Daddies *have* to say that," said Paulie Allen Puffer. "That's so you'll go to sleep at night and not bother them."

He squinted his eyes at me.

"Why do you think daddies and mommies sleep together in the same room, anyway? It's so they can *protect* each other from the monster. Or else their heads might get chewed off."

Just then, I wrinkled up my nose at that terrible thought. Then I hanged out my tongue. And I did a sick face.

And guess what?

The cheese man took the class picture.

2

Just Say *Right!*

After school pictures, we went back to Room Nine.

I put my head down on my table.

"There's no such things as monsters. There's no such things as monsters," I whispered to just myself. "'Cause my very own daddy told me that. And he wouldn't even lie to me...probably."

Mrs. said for me to sit up in my chair.

She passed out work for us to do.

It was called printing our letters. Only

I didn't actually feel like doing that.

I tapped on my bestest friend named Lucille.

"Guess what, Lucille? There's no such things as monsters. There's really, really not. And so a monster doesn't even live under my bed, probably. Right, Lucille? Right? Right?"

"Shh! I'm doing my letters," she said.

"Yes, Lucille. I *know* you are doing your letters. Only I just wanted to tell you about the monster. 'Cause he's not even real …right?"

Lucille didn't say *right*.

"How come you're not saying *right*, Lucille? Just say *right*. Okay? Just say *monsters aren't real*. And I won't even bother you anymore."

All of a sudden, Lucille did a mad breath.

"*Now* look what you made me do, Junie B.! You made me ruin my big G! I *told* you not to bother me!"

She quick grabbed her paper and runned to Mrs. to fix it.

I tapped my fingers on my table.

Then I turned around and looked behind me.

I smiled at a boy named crybaby William.

"Guess what, William. There's no such things as monsters. And so a monster doesn't even live under my bed, probably. Right? William? Right? Right?"

William moved his seat away from me.

I followed him in my chair.

"I'm right, don't you think, William? A monster really *doesn't* live under my bed, does he? Plus also, he doesn't put my head in his mouth."

William slided his chair away some more.

I scooted after him.

"Just say *right*. Okay, William? Just say there's not a monster under my bed. And I will be on my way."

William picked up his chair. He carried it all the way to the middle of the floor.

That's how come I had to carry my chair to the middle of the floor, too.

I sat down and smiled very sweet.

"Right, William? I'm right, aren't I?" I said.

Only too bad for me. 'Cause just then I felt hands on my shoulders.

I looked up.

It was Mrs.

I did a gulp.

"Hello. How are you today?" I said kind of nervous.

Mrs. zoomed my chair back to my table.

It was not fun.

I quick picked up my pencil.

"Guess what? I am going to do my work now," I said. "Plus also, I am not even going to talk. 'Cause I don't actually like anyone in this area."

Mrs. tapped her foot at me.

"Love your shoes," I said real soft.

Her foot kept tapping.

Only just then, a very great thing happened. And it is called, the bell rang for the end of school!

I hurried up out the door.

Then me and my other bestest friend named Grace runned to the bus together.

"Grace! Grace! Guess what? There's no such things as monsters! And so I don't even have one under my bed, probably. Right, Grace? Right?"

That Grace didn't say *right*.

That's how come I grabbed her by her shoulders. And I jiggled and jiggled her. 'Cause I was fed up with these people, that's why.

"How come you won't say *right*, Grace?

17

How come nobody will say *right*? 'Cause I'm getting at the end of my rope with this thing!"

That Grace took my hands off of her.

"I can't say *right,* because a monster really *might* live under your bed, Junie B.," she said.

My eyes got big and wide at her.

"No, Grace! No! Do not say that! Do not say a monster might live under my bed! 'Cause that cannot even be true. Or else I would have spotted that guy by now!"

"No, you wouldn't," she said. "My big sister said that monsters can turn theirselves invisible when you look at them. And so that's how come nobody ever sees them."

That Grace looked serious at me.

"That makes sense, don't you think? Huh, Junie B.? Right?"

Just then, my throat got dry. And my stomach got the shakies.

I looked out the window very upset.

And I didn't say *right*.

3

The Invisiblest Guy

I ran in my house and hollered for my grandma Helen Miller.

"GRANDMA MILLER! GRANDMA HELEN MILLER! I AM SO GLAD TO BE HOME! 'CAUSE TODAY WAS NOT A VERY GOOD DAY AT MY SCHOOL!"

Grandma Miller was in the kitchen. She was holding my baby brother named Ollie.

I jumped up and down in front of her.

"PICK ME UP! PICK ME UP! PICK ME UP!"

"I can't right now, Toots," she said. "I've got my hands full with Ollie."

"Yeah, only put him on the floor," I said. "'Cause I need a hug down here, Helen."

Grandma Miller leaned down and hugged me.

She said don't call her Helen.

"Why don't you go change your clothes?" she said. "Then you and I will make some popcorn. And you can tell me all about your day. How does that sound?"

Just then, my whole face got happy. 'Cause popcorn is my most favorite thing in the whole wide world!

"Hurray!" I shouted. "Hurray for pop-corn!"

I ran right to my room. Then I took off

my shoes and socks. And my feet did a happy dance on the floor. It was called the Happy Feet Popcorn Dance.

They danced around and around. Also, they jumped on my bed. And they springed to the floor. And they did a giant twirly on my rug.

I clapped my hands real joyful.

"Grandma! Hey, Grandma! Guess what? I am having a good time in here! And so I am not even thinking about the monster under my bed!"

Just then, I did a gulp.

'Cause I shouldn't have said that, I think.

I looked at my bed kind of nervous.

What if the monster was under there right this very minute?

And what if he was looking at my piggy toes?

And what if he wanted to *eat* them?

"Oh no," I said. "Oh no. Oh no. 'Cause piggy toes look just like little wiener sausages, I think."

I freezed right where I was standing.

"GRANDMA MILLER! GRANDMA MILLER! COME QUICK! I NEED YOU!" I shouted.

Grandma Miller flied to my room. Then she picked me up. And she hugged me real tight.

"What on *earth* is the trouble?" she asked.

She sat down with me on my bed.

"NO, GRANDMA! NO! NO! WE CAN'T SIT HERE!"

I squeezed out of her arms and ran out my door.

"THERE'S A MONSTER UNDER MY BED!" I yelled.

I jumped up and down.

"RUN, HELEN! RUN LIKE THE WIND!"

Only Grandma Helen Miller didn't run. She just flopped back on my covers. And she closed her eyes.

"No, Junie B. *Please*. We're not going to go through this monster business again, are we? We've talked about monsters before, remember? We decided that there are no such things as monsters."

"Yes, but I have new information," I said. "'Cause the monster under my bed turns himself invisible whenever we look at him. Plus at night—after my eyes are closed—he climbs next to me. And he puts my head in his mouth."

Grandma Miller did a big breath. Then she went to the kitchen. And she brought back my daddy's flashlight.

She shined it under my bed.

"No monster, Junie B. *None*. I don't see one single monster under this bed," she said.

"See?" I said. "That proves it, Grandma! He turned himself invisible!"

Grandma Miller shook her head.

"No, Junie B. The monster did *not* turn himself invisible. The monster is simply not *there*. He does not *exist*. Period."

"Yes, he does, Grandma! He does *too* exist. 'Cause Paulie Allen Puffer's big brother even said so. Plus also I've seen the drool."

Grandma Miller said to calm down my voice. She got me a drink of water.

"Why don't we forget about the monster for now, and we'll go make popcorn. You can talk to your mother about this when she gets home. I bet Mother will know exactly what to do."

I thought and thought.

"What, Grandma? What will she do?" I asked.

Then—all of a sudden—a light bulb went on in my head.

"Hey! *I* know what she'll do! Mother will get the broom and bash the monster's head in! 'Cause I saw her do that to a roach before! And she is excellent at it!"

Grandma Miller closed her eyes again.

She said I am a strange one.

27

4

Spooky and Scary

Pretty soon, Mother came home from work.

I zoomed to her speedy quick. And handed her the broom.

"MOTHER! MOTHER! COME ON! COME ON! LET'S GO! LET'S GO GET THE MONSTER!" I hollered.

Mother turned her head real slow. And she looked at Grandma Miller.

Grandma sucked in her cheeks.

"A monster," she said kind of quiet. "Under the bed. We've been waiting for you to come home, so you can bash its head in."

I tugged on her sweater.

"Plus tell her about the drool, Grandma!" I said.

But Grandma Miller headed to the door. And she said the words *I'm outta here.*

I pulled on Mother's arm.

"Come on! Come on, Mother! The monster's really real! 'Cause Paulie Allen Puffer told me everybody has a monster under the bed! Plus that Grace said it can turn *invisible.* And so that is how come we never saw that guy before."

Mother sat down at the kitchen table. And she lifted me onto her lap.

Then she said that Paulie Allen Puffer was just trying to scare me. Plus that Grace didn't know what she was talking about.

"There is *no* monster under your bed,

Junie B. I promise you. Monsters are *not* real," she said.

"Yes, they are! They are too real! 'Cause Paulie Allen Puffer's brother even said so! And he is in seventh grade! And he said monsters crawl on your bed! And they fit your head in their mouth! And so that is where the drool comes from! 'Cause I am not even a baby!"

Just then, I heard the front door open.

It was my daddy! He was home from work, too!

"Daddy, Daddy! There's a monster under my bed! Only you said monsters aren't real. But they really, really are!"

I pulled on his arm.

"Come on, Daddy! Let's get him!"

Daddy looked at Mother a real long time.

They went in the hall and did whispering.

Pretty soon, Daddy came back to me.

He said we would look for the monster after dinner. But first we would cook some hamburgers on the grill.

"Oh boy!" I said. "Oh boy! 'Cause hamburgers are my most favorite things in the whole wide world! Plus also I like pasketti and meatballs."

After that, me and Daddy went outside.

He got a flipper for the hamburgers. Then he gave me a flipper, too. 'Cause I am old enough, that's why.

I runned all over with that thing.

I flipped a rock and a flower and a dirt ball. Plus also, I flipped a dead lizard I found in the driveway.

Then Mother took my flipper away.

'Cause I am not old enough, that's why.

After dinner I took my bath.

Then Mother and Daddy read me a

story. And they hugged me good night.

"See you in the morning," said Mother.

"See you in the morning," said Daddy.

I sat up in my bed.

"Yeah, only I can't even sleep in here. 'Cause you guys didn't bash that monster yet."

Daddy rubbed his tired eyes.

"There's *no* monster, Junie B. There is *nothing* to be afraid of," he said.

Then he kissed me. And he went out of my room. And Mother went with him.

I quick got out of bed and followed those two.

They turned around and spotted me.

"Hello. How are you today?" I said very pleasant. "I am going to sit in the kitchen and not bother anyone. Plus also, I might watch Eyewitness News at Ten."

Mother carried me back to bed.

I followed her out again.

"Want to bake a lemon pie? A lemon pie would be fun, don't you think?" I asked.

This time, Mother marched me back to my room real fast.

"Do *not* get up again, Junie B.," she said. "Enough is enough."

I waited for her feet to walk away.

Then I tippytoed to my baby brother's room. And I climbed into his crib.

It was very crowded in there.

That's how come I had to get out and put baby Ollie on the floor.

Then I climbed in his crib again. And I pulled up the blanket all warm and cozy.

Only too bad for me, 'cause just then

that crybaby baby started to scream.

Daddy runned into the room speedy quick.

He turned on the light and saw me.

I did a gulp.

"Hello. How are you today?" I said kind of nervous. "I am all warm and cozy."

Daddy quick swished me out of there.

Then he put baby Ollie back in the crib.

And he took me to my bed again.

"Okay. This is *it*," he grouched. "This is the *last* time I want to have to come in here. Do you understand, missy? Do *not* get out of this bed *one more time*."

I started to cry a teeny bit.

"Yeah, only what about the monster?" I said. "'Cause he is still under my bed, I think."

Daddy throwed his hands in the air.

Then he turned on my light. And he looked for the monster all over the place.

First, he looked under my bed. Then he looked in my closet. And in my drawers. And in my trash can. Plus also, he looked in my crayon box.

"*No* monster, Junie B.," he said. "No monster anywhere. You're going to have to believe me. Monsters are *not* real!"

He sat down on my bed.

"I'm going to go now," he said. "I'm going to leave your door open. And I'm going to leave the hall light on. But this is it, okay? You have to trust me, Junie B. There is *no* monster under your bed."

I holded onto his shirt.

"Yeah, only tuck in my sheets. Okay? Tuck them in real tight. Or else my feet might hang over the side. And piggy toes look like little wiener sausages."

Daddy tucked in my sheets. "There. Now good night."

"Yeah, only get my teddy. Okay, Daddy? Plus also get my Raggedy Ann named Ruth. And my Raggedy Andy named Larry. And get my stuffed elephant named Philip Johnny Bob."

Daddy got all those guys for me. He tucked them in my bed.

"There. That's *it*. Now good night," he said.

He walked right out of my room. And he kept on going down the hall.

I looked all around in the dark.

It was spooky and scary in there.

"PHILIP JOHNNY BOB WANTS A DRINK OF WATER!" I shouted out real loud.

I waited and waited.

"YEAH, ONLY HE REALLY, REALLY NEEDS ONE! ON ACCOUNT OF HE IS HAVING A PROBLEM WITH HIS TRUNK!"

Daddy didn't come.

"RAGGEDY RUTH NEEDS A KLEENEX!" I yelled next.

After that, my voice got quieter.

"Raggedy Larry wants a cookie," I said.

But still Daddy didn't come.

5
My Worstest Night Ever

It was my worstest night ever.

I didn't sleep any winks.

That's because I had to keep my eyes open. Or else the monster wouldn't stay invisible.

I heard Mother and Daddy go to bed.

"GOOD NIGHT, EVERYBODY! GOOD NIGHT! IT'S ME! IT'S JUNIE B. JONES! I AM STILL AWAKE IN HERE. 'CAUSE I CAN'T EVEN CLOSE MY EYES OR

THE MONSTER WILL COME!"

Mother and Daddy didn't yell back.

"PLUS HERE'S ANOTHER THING I NEED TO TELL YOU! DON'T TURN OUT THE HALL LIGHT. PLUS DON'T SHUT MY DOOR! PLUS DON'T SHUT YOUR DOOR, EITHER!"

"Go to sleep!" grouched Mother.

I smiled very relieved.

"It was good to hear your voice," I said kind of quiet.

After that, Mother and Daddy got in bed. And they turned out their light.

Daddy started to snore.

"Oh no," I said. "Now he won't even be awake to save me if the monster comes."

I pulled Philip Johnny Bob out of my covers.

"*I will save you,*" he said. "*I will squirt water in the monster's face. Plus I will stomple him with my giant elephant feet. And so now you can close your eyes. And you don't even have to worry about that guy.*"

I looked and looked at him.

"Yeah, only here's the problem," I said. "You're not actually strong 'cause you just have fluffy in you. Plus also you can't really squirt water. And so who am I kidding here?"

Philip Johnny Bob stared at me a real long time.

Then he went back under the covers.

All of a sudden I heard feet in the hall.

It was monster feet, I think!

They kept getting closer and closer to me.

Then pretty soon they runned right in my room!

And guess what?

It was my dog, Tickle! That's what!

"Tickle! Tickle! I am so glad to see you! 'Cause now you can protect me from the monster! And so why didn't I think of this before?"

I pulled back my covers and patted for him to jump up.

"Here, Tickle! You can sleep right on my pillow! 'Cause Mother won't even find out about this!"

Tickle springed right up there. He runned all around on my bed.

He put his head under my sheets and runned down to my feet.

"No, Tickle! No! No! You have to come back up here! Or else how will you even protect me?"

I pulled him back up.

He put his paws on Raggedy Larry. And chewed his red hair.

"No, Tickle! No! No!" I said.

Just then, Tickle springed over me. And he landed on my elephant named Philip Johnny Bob.

He holded him by his trunk. And shaked that guy all around.

I saved Philip Johnny Bob just in time.

Then I pushed Tickle off my bed. And he runned out of my room.

Philip Johnny Bob was very upset.

I petted his trunk.

Also, I hugged Raggedy Larry.

Only too bad for me. 'Cause just then Raggedy Ruth fell right out of my bed. On account of the dumb sheets weren't tucked in anymore.

Me and Raggedy Larry peeked over the side at her.

"*Get her,*" said Raggedy Larry.

"Yeah, only I *can't* get her," I said real upset. "Or else the monster will grab my hand and pull me right under the bed."

I thought about what to do.

Then—all of a sudden—I picked up all my friends in my arms.

"We have to make a run for it," I told them. "We have to sleep with Mother and Daddy tonight. 'Cause we will be safe with them. Plus they won't even know we're there probably. 'Cause their bed is the size of a king."

I stood on the side of my bed. Then I jumped way out to the middle of the floor. And I quick picked up Raggedy Ruth.

I ran to Mother and Daddy's room.

They were sleeping and snoring.

"Shh," I said to Raggedy Larry.

"Shh," I said to Philip Johnny Bob.

Then all of us crawled down the middle of their bed. And we sneaked under their covers.

Only too bad for me. 'Cause Mother rolled right over on Philip Johnny Bob's trunk. And it waked her right up.

She turned on the light.

I did a gulp.

"Hello. How are you today? Me and my friends are sleeping here. 'Cause we didn't think you'd mind, probably."

Mother carried me back to my room zippity quick.

Then she leaned close to my ear. And she talked very scary with her teeth closed.

"Do...*not*...get...out...of...bed...one...
more...time," she said.

And so guess what?

I didn't.

6

Flatsos

The next day at school, I was pooped and tired.

I opened one eye with my fingers. And I drawed a picture for art.

It did not turn out that professional.

After that, I holded up my head with my hands. And I waited for school to be over.

Me and that Grace rode home on the bus together.

I yawned and yawned.

"Darn it, Grace. I wish you never even

told me that monsters can turn invisible. 'Cause now I can't even close my eyes at night."

"I can," said that Grace. "That's because I don't have a monster under my bed anymore. My mom figured out how to get rid of it."

My eyes got big and wide.

"How, Grace? How did she do that?"

"Easy," said that Grace. "First, she sucked it up in the vacuum cleaner. Then she put the vacuum cleaner bag in the trash compactor. And she squished the monster into a *flatso*."

Just then, I hugged and hugged that girl! 'Cause that was brilliant, of course!

"Thank you, Grace! Thank you! Thank you! 'Cause I have a vacuum cleaner right in my very own home! And so I can do that too, probably!"

After I got off my bus, I zoomed to my house speedy fast.

"GRANDMA MILLER! GRANDMA MILLER! I KNOW HOW TO GET RID OF THE MONSTER!" I hollered.

Then I runned to the closet and got Mother's vacuum cleaner. And I pulled that big thing all the way to my room.

Grandma Miller came to my door.

I told her all about how to get rid of the monster. And guess what? She was a good sport about it!

First, she plugged the vacuum cleaner right into my wall. Then she put it under the bed. And she sucked the monster right out of there!

"HURRAY! HURRAY! YOU GOT HIM! YOU GOT THE MONSTER, GRANDMA!" I yelled real thrilled.

Grandma Miller runned with the bag to the kitchen. And she throwed it in the trash can.

"There. That ought to do the trick," she said very happy.

I looked and looked at the trash.

Then I did a teeny frown.

"Yeah, only here's the problem, Grandma. You didn't actually put the bag in the trash compactor. And that is what turns the monster into a flatso."

Grandma Miller smiled.

"Yes, but this house doesn't *have* a trash compactor, Junie B.," she said. "*Your* monster will just have to stay in the vacuum cleaner bag."

My frown got bigger.

"Yeah, but what if he leaks out, Grandma? Then maybe he might float in the air. All the way back to my room.

And he will get under my bed again."

Grandma Miller tapped on the counter with her fingers. Then her cheeks filled up with air. And she let it out real slow.

"Okay…how 'bout this? What if I take it outside? I'll take the bag outside. And I'll push it way down in the big garbage can. And then I'll press the lid down really tight, so he can't get out."

"Yeah, but he still won't be a flatso," I said very whining.

Just then, Grandma Miller got fusstration in her.

She grabbed the vacuum cleaner bag and ran outside.

Then she put it on the driveway.

And she got in her car.

And she backed up over that thing with her tires.

Pretty soon, she came back in the house.

She brushed her hands together.

"There! *Now* he's a flatso!" she said kind of growly.

After she left, I got on the couch. And I stared very nervous at the driveway.

'Cause guess why?

A car is not a trash compactor.

That's why.

7

Snarlies and Snufflies

That night, I heard snarlies under my bed.

Mother said it was my 'magination.

"No, it is *not* my 'magination," I said. "I can hear snarlies. Plus also I hear snories and snufflies and droolies."

Mother rolled her eyes way up at the ceiling.

"Honestly, Junie B....where in the *world* do you get this stuff?" she asked.

I thought and thought.

"It just automatically comes in my head," I said. "It is a gift, I think."

After that, I begged to sleep in her bed.

But Mother said no.

Then Daddy said no, too.

"You have to trust us, Junie B.," he said. "We would never let anything hurt you. There's nothing in your room to be afraid of."

And so that's how come I had to sleep in my own bed. For the whole entire night.

Plus also, I had to sleep there the next night. And the next night. And the next night after that, too.

That was the night when the worst thing of all happened.

'Cause I accidentally sleeped too much. And the monster must have crawled on my bed. 'Cause in the morning there was drool on my pillow!

I screamed very loud when I felt it.

"HELP! HELP! THERE'S DROOL! THERE'S DROOL! I *TOLD* YOU THIS WOULD HAPPEN! I *TOLD* YOU THE MONSTER WOULD COME!"

I ran in Mother and Daddy's room and showed them my pillow.

Mother holded her head.

"When is this *ever* going to end?" she said. "When are you *ever* going to realize that there are *no such things* as monsters?"

She did not wait for me to answer.

"*Everyone* drools on their pillow sometimes," she said. "It doesn't mean you're a baby. Your mouth just opens when you're sleeping. And you drool a little bit. It's no big deal. And it is *not* from monsters!"

After that, she went out of her room to the kitchen. And Daddy went to get Ollie.

I crawled into her bed and counted my piggy toes.

Good news.

There was ten.

That day at kindergarten, Mrs. had a surprise for us.

It was called our school pictures were
back from the cheese man.

She passed them out to us.

Lucille got hers first.

My eyes popped out at those things!

"Lucille! Look how gorgeous they are!
They are the gorgeousest pictures I ever
saw!" I said.

Lucille fluffed her fluffy dress.

"I know it. I know they are gorgeous.
That's just how I look, Junie B. I can't even
help it."

After that, Lucille stood up at the table.

And she held up her pictures for everyone to
see.

Mrs. said *sit down* to her.

Just then, Mrs. bended down next to me.
And she smoothed my hair.

"Junie B., honey? You might want to
have *your* pictures taken again," she said
kind of quiet.

Then she handed me my envelope

real secret. So nobody could see.

I sneaked a peek at those things.

My stomach felt sickish inside.

"I look like I smelled stink," I said.

I quick tried to hide my pictures. But Lucille grabbed them away from me.

"Eeew! Gross!" she said. "Junie B. looks gross!"

I tried to grab them back.

"YEAH, ONLY THESE ARE NOT EVEN YOUR BEESWAX, MADAM!" I yelled very mad.

Only too bad for me. 'Cause lots of other kids already saw them. And they laughed and laughed at those things.

Finally I grabbed the pictures back. And I hided them in my coat.

I didn't talk to Room Nine for the whole rest of the day.

8
Scary-face Me!

After I got home from school, I sat on my bed. And I looked at my pictures.

"I hate these ugly, dumb things!" I said very furious. "These are the ugliest dumb pictures I ever even saw!"

I leaned over the edge and holded a picture down there.

"See this? See this, you stupid monster? This picture is just as scary as you! And so maybe I might put it right under my bed!

And it will scare your whole entire pants off!"

Just then, I sat up very straight.

'Cause that might be a good idea I just thought of!

I quick found my scissors.

Then I cut my school pictures apart from each other. And I shoved them right under my bed.

"I am not even afraid of you, you dumb monster! 'Cause these ugly pictures can bite your head off!"

Just then, I heard Mother come home from work.

"Mother! Mother! My pictures came! My pictures came!" I hollered very thrilled.

She hurried up to my room.

I pointed under my bed.

"See them, Mother? See my school pictures? I spread them out under there."

Mother looked curious at me.

She bended down and picked up a picture.

Her mouth did a gasp.

"Oh my," she whispered.

I clapped and clapped.

"I know they are *oh my*! That is why I put them under my bed! Get it, Mother? Get it? Now my scary face will be down there all the time! And so that monster already got scared away, I bet!"

All of a sudden, Mother started to laugh.

Then I started to laugh, too.

Plus here's another happy thing. 'Cause this morning there was more drool on my pillow.

Only I am not that worried.

'Cause it was from Raggedy Ruth, I bet.

Or else maybe it was from Philip Johnny Bob.

Or maybe it was even from me.

But that does not mean I'm a baby.

'Cause *everybody* drools on their pillow once in a while!

My very own mother told me that.

And she would not even lie to me...

probably.

Laugh yourself silly with

ALL the Junie B. Jones books!

Laugh yourself silly with
junie b. jones®

Join the

Got to b...
junie b.®!
KIDS' READING CLUB

for Junie B. news, book samplers, games, jokes, and more!

1083a   **JunieBKidsClub.com**

Don't miss this next book about my fun in kindergarten!

Someone took Junie B.'s new black mitttens. So when she finds a wonderful pen, she should be allowed to keep it, too. Right?

Available Now!

Read these other great books by Barbara Park!